Dear Parent:
Your child's love of reading starts here!

Every child learns to read in a different way and at his or her own speed. Some go back and forth between reading levels and read favorite books again and again. Others read through each level in order. You can help your young reader improve and become more confident by encouraging his or her own interests and abilities. From books your child reads with you to the first books he or she reads alone, there are I Can Read Books for every stage of reading:

SHARED READING
Basic language, word repetition, and whimsical illustrations, ideal for sharing with your emergent reader

BEGINNING READING
Short sentences, familiar words, and simple concepts for children eager to read on their own

READING WITH HELP
Engaging stories, longer sentences, and language play for developing readers

READING ALONE
Complex plots, challenging vocabulary, and high-interest topics for the independent reader

ADVANCED READING
Short paragraphs, chapters, and exciting themes for the perfect bridge to chapter books

I Can Read Books have introduced children to the joy of reading since 1957. Featuring award-winning authors and illustrators and a fabulous cast of beloved characters, I Can Read Books set the standard for beginning readers.

A lifetime of discovery begins with the magical words **"I Can Read!"**

*Visit www.icanread.com for information
on enriching your child's reading experience.*

SNOWBALL SOUP

BY MERCER MAYER

HarperCollinsPublishers

To Grant and Christian Hade

HarperCollins®, 📕®, and I Can Read Book® are trademarks of HarperCollins Publishers.

Library of Congress catalog card number: 2006939824
ISBN 978-0-06-083544-6 (trade bdg.) — ISBN 978-0-06-083543-9 (pbk.)

10   11   12   13   SCP   10   9   8   7   6   5   4   ❖   First Edition

A Big Tuna Trading Company LLC/J. R. Sansevere Book
www.littlecritter.com

I am Little Critter.

This is Little Sister.

She is my little sister.

That is Dog.

He is our dog.

Wow! Look at all the snow!

Dog likes snow.

Little Sister likes snow.

I like snow, too.

We play in the snow.

I dig in the snow.

Little Sister rolls in the snow.

We make snowballs.

We throw snowballs.

Oops!

Sorry, Little Sister.

We make a snowman.

We roll some big snowballs.

One, two, three.

One snowball on the bottom.

The next one goes on top.

This one goes on the very top.
Ta-da!

Little Sister puts on the hat.

I put on the nose.

Dog puts on the arms.

Then we put on the eyes.

Hello, Snowman!

Time for lunch, Snowman!

What does a snowman eat?

Snowball soup!

We make a pot of

snowball soup.

We give the snowman a spoon.

Eat all your soup, Snowman!

We go inside.

We eat soup for lunch, too!

Yum! Yum!

Thank you, Mom!

We go outside.

Oh, no! Dog is eating
the snowball soup.

Silly dog!

Snowball soup is not for dogs.

That was for the snowman.

Don't worry, Snowman!

30

Time to make more
snowball soup.
Yum! Yum!

31